HIAWYN ORAM worked as a copywriter before she began to write for children in 1979. Since then she has written more than forty children's books. Her previous titles include *Angry Arthur* (Anderson Press), *Just Like Us* and *Billy and the Babysitter* (Orchard Books). She has also collaborated with the composer, Carl Davies, on two musicals for children. Her previous books for Frances Lincoln are *Mine!* and *Little Brother and the Cough*, both illustrated by Mary Rees. Hiawyn has two sons and lives in South London.

LUCY SU started working as an illustrator while still at Brighton Art School but she became interested in children's books after the birth of her first child. Since then she has illustrated many picture books, teen books and board books. *Peekaboo Friends!* was her first book for Frances Lincoln. Lucy lives with her family in Teddington.

For little John G and his mum ~ *H.O.*
For Wilkie Duncan Morrison ~ *L.S.*

First published in Great Britain in 2003 by
Frances Lincoln Limited, 4 Torriano Mews,
Torriano Avenue, London NW5 2RZ

www.franceslincoln.com

First paperback edition 2004

British Library Cataloguing in Publication Data
available on request

ISBN 0-7112-2110-3

Printed in Singapore

3 5 7 9 8 6 4 2

The Best Party
Of Them All

HIAWYN ORAM
Illustrated by LUCY SU

FRANCES LINCOLN

Katie and Harry were twins.
They wanted it to be their birthday.

They wished and wished it was,
but it wasn't.

It was their friend Tim's birthday.
This was the invitation to his party.

You are invited to a Dinosaur Party!
Date: Saturday   Time: 11.30 – 2.00pm
Dress: Jurassic Park   Place: The Museum
Food: pine-needle burgers, fir-cone fries,
swamp jelly

"We want a Dinosaur Party when it's our birthday," said Harry.

"With pine-needle burgers and swamp jelly," said Katie.

Then they dressed up...

and went to the party and forgot it wasn't
their birthday because they had such a...

megasauric time.

But when the next invitation came
it still wasn't their birthday.
It was Mary's.

Please come
to my party
It's going to be
a
Circus
Date: Sunday
Time: 2.00 p.m.
Place: My house
Dress: for the
Big Top

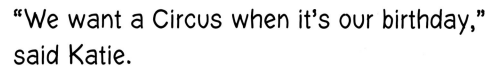

"We want a Circus when it's our birthday," said Katie.
  "With a Big Top and Tickle the Clown," said Harry.
Then they dressed up...

and went to the party and forgot it wasn't
their birthday because they had such a...

silly time.

But when the next invitation came
it still wasn't their birthday.
It was Nicola's.

To: Katie
and Harry

It's my **B**irthday
&
you are invited
to a
Picnic in the **P**ark

On: Friday at 1.00p.m.
At: The Ponds in the Park
Dress: Woodland Creatures
Food: Ant sandwiches, ladybird
cakes, squashed wasp biscuits

"When it's our birthday, we want
a Picnic in the Park," said Harry.
   "With Ant sandwiches and Ladybird
cakes, but NO wasps," said Katie.
Then they dressed up…

and went to the party and forgot it wasn't
their birthday because they had such a...

wonderfully wild time.

But when the next invitation came
it STILL wasn't their birthday.
It was Halloween and George
was having a party.

You are invited to a
HALLOWEEN PARTY
Date: Saturday
Place: bottom of the garden!
Parents: welcome (with magic spells!)
Going Home Presents: spelling books!
Time: After dark!
Food: Pumpkin soup, Dracula cake!
Dress- witches, ghosts, black cats

"When it's our birthday we want
a Halloween Party," said Harry.
  "With pumpkins and witches even
if it's not Halloween," said Katie.
Then they dressed up...

and went to the party and forgot it wasn't
their birthday because they had such a...

whoOO... scary time!

But when the NEXT invitation came...
there were ten of them and they
were BLANK.

"Now," said their mum, "what do you think
these are for?"
    "OUR PARTY!" cried the Twins.
"Hurry, write in OUR PARTY!"

So their mum wrote...

You are invited to
THE TWINS' PARTY
On Friday at 2 o'clock
at 4 Rockery Drive

And when the day came, they were
so excited they could hardly dress

because it wasn't a Dinosaur Party, it wasn't
a Circus Party, it wasn't a Picnic Party,
it wasn't a Halloween Party...

it was THEIR party.   More than **megasauric**

sillier than
silly

wilder than **wonderfully wild**

scarier than just
whoOO... scary

and for Katie and Harry it was easily...

THE BEST PARTY OF THEM ALL!

MORE TITLES IN PAPERBACK
FROM FRANCES LINCOLN

MINE!

Hiawyn Oram
Illustrated by Mary Rees

Isabel went to play with Claudia. She climbed on to Claudia's
rocking horse. 'Mine!' shrieked Claudia and pushed her off.
Poor Isabel has a hard time trying to play with her friend,
but it is Isabel who gets the last laugh.

ISBN 0-7112-0682-1

LITTLE BROTHER AND THE COUGH

Hiawyn Oram
Illustrated by Mary Rees

When a new baby brother arrives in the family,
it's not always easy. In this case, it leads to a Cough,
a very Bad Cough, a very very VERY Bad Cough!

ISBN 0-7112-0845-X

I WANT A PET

Lauren Child

I really want a pet. But what sort of pet should it be?
Perhaps an African lion, but they have a habit of snacking
between meals. Perhaps a boa constrictor, but they squeeze
a little too tightly. There must be a pet that won't leave
footprints, doesn't eat, doesn't move and doesn't make a peep.

ISBN 0-7112-1339-9

Frances Lincoln titles are available from all good bookshops.
You can also buy books and find out more about your favourite titles,
authors and illustrators on our website: www.franceslincoln.com.